this book belongs to

We wanted to share a helpful tip with you to ensure that your coloring experience is as smooth and enjoyable as possible. If you plan on using markers to color in the book, we recommend placing a blank sheet of paper under your artwork. This will prevent any bleed-through onto the other pages and help preserve the quality of your coloring book.

Thank you again for choosing our coloring book. We hope it brings a touch of magic to your day. Best regards, oh my publishing.

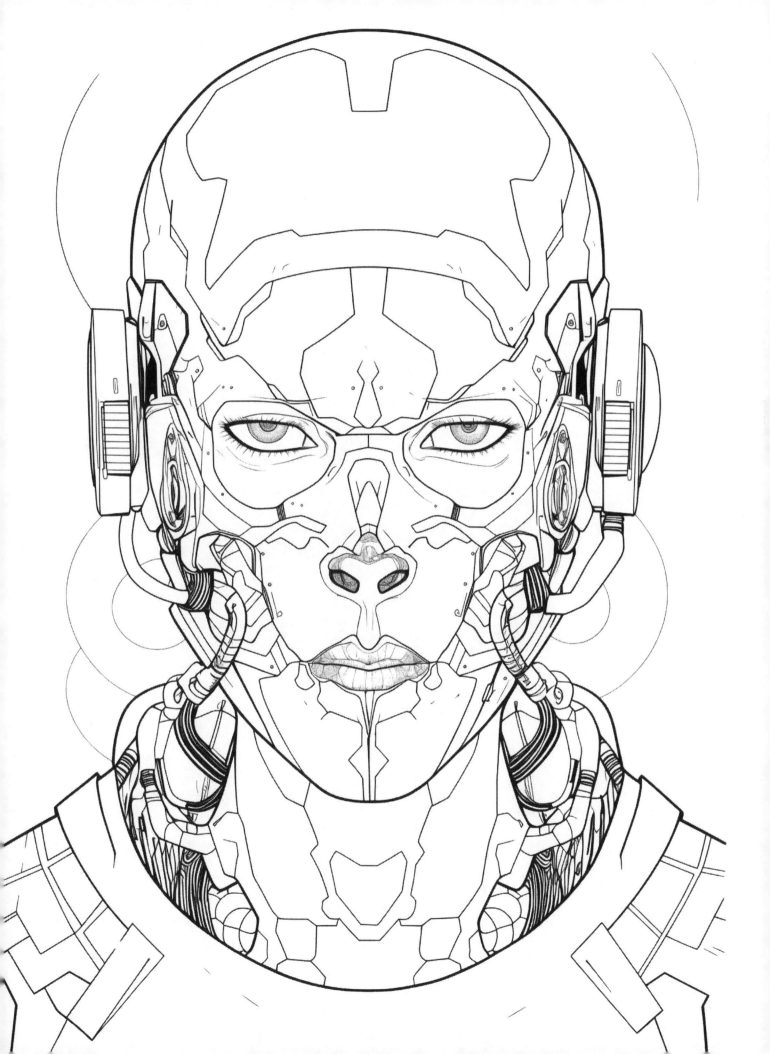

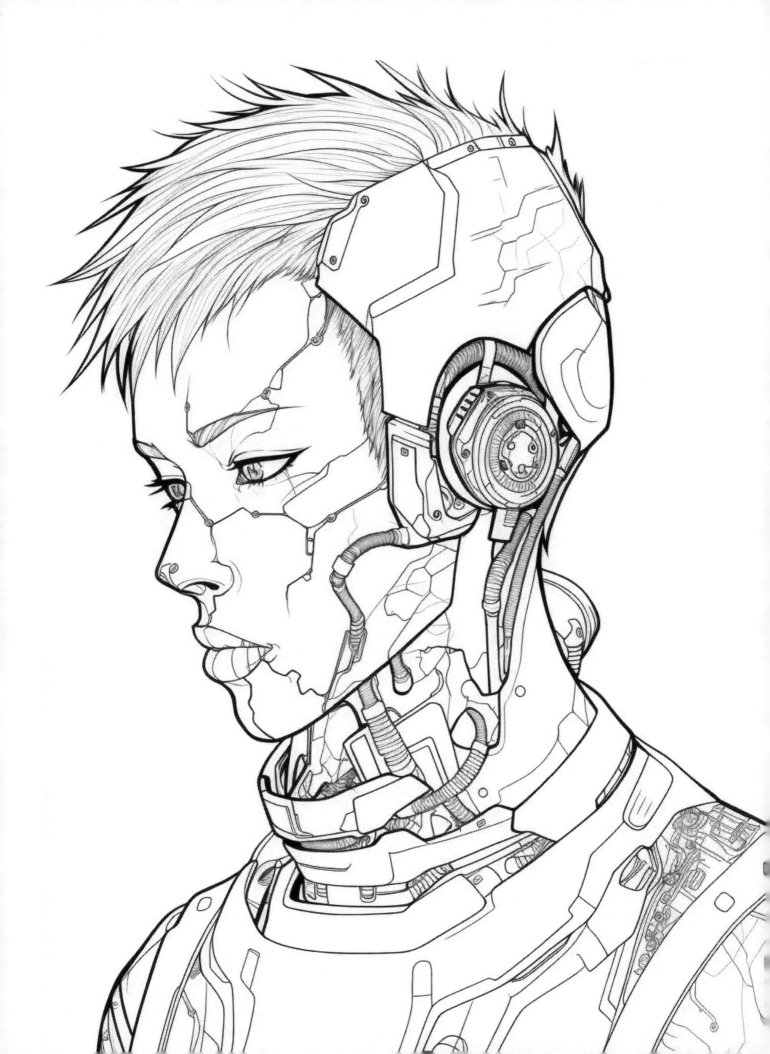

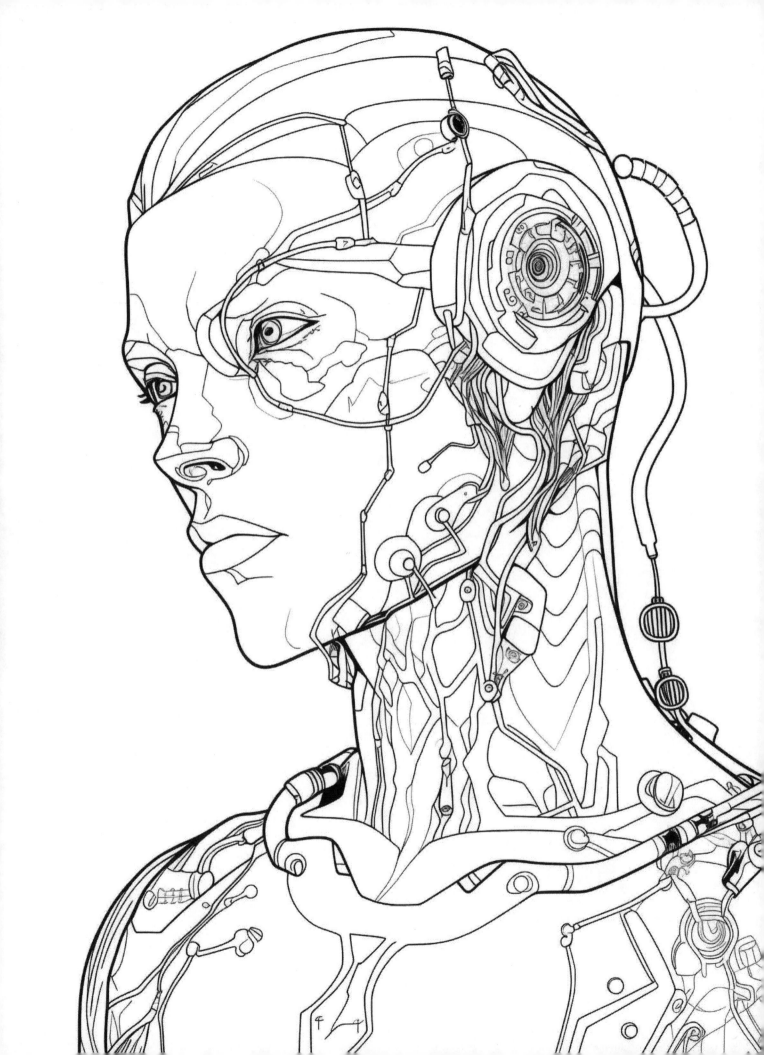

Dear customer

Thank you so much for your recent purchase of our coloring book. We hope that it brings you many hours of joy and creativity as you color and trace your way through its pages.

As a small business, we rely on the support and feedback of customers like you to help us grow and improve. We would be so grateful if you could take just a few moments to leave a review of our coloring book on Amazon. Your honest feedback will not only help us continue to improve our products, but it will also help other customers make informed decisions about their purchases.

We know that your time is valuable, and we truly appreciate any feedback you can provide. Your words have the power to make a difference, and we are committed to using your feedback to create even better products in the future.

Thank you again for choosing our coloring book, and for taking the time to consider leaving a review. We are honored to have you as a customer, and we look forward to hearing from you soon.

If you like this you may also like

SCAN ME FOR
THESE
COLORING
BOOKS!

SCAN ME FOR
THESE
COLORING
BOOKS!

to purchase any of these just type the title into amazon or go to
https://www.amazon.com/stores/my-goodness-
publishing/author/B0C2SZF7XS or to
https://www.amazon.com/stores/oh-my-publishing/author/B0C3G6YXWY

Made in United States
Orlando, FL
20 December 2024

56124448R00054